This book belongs to: _____

My Kitty's name is: _____

Anything
is
PAWsible!

I dedicate this book to my Daddy God.
He restores, renews, rebuilds, and rePURRposes
every broken place in my life.

I also dedicate this book to everyone who has ever felt abandoned,
scared, or alone. May you find your community and belonging, may
you help those in need, and may you snuggle down deep in the
lap of LOVE and reflect on the beauty of everyday miracles.

A very special Thank MEW to my Title Sponsor—**Jeff Crilley and the Real News PR Team**
You guys are the best in the biz! Ya'll have been my tribe for the past year. You give me
insPURRation and allow me to be ridiculous and do interMEWs as Instagram Cat Mom.
realnewspr.com

The Christmas Kitten
by **Jessica Spawn**
© 2017 Hungry Cat Media, LLC

**HUNGRY CAT
MEDIA, LLC**

For more information, email **jess@hungrycatmedia.com**.
HungryCatMedia.com | **InstagramCatMom.com**

Illustrated by **Benjamin Vincent** | **benvincent.com**
Edited by **Amy Betz** | **tinytalesediting.com**
Title Design, Typeset, and Layout by **Paul and Katrina Sirmon** | **buzzbombcreative.com**

ISBN-13: 978-1979931335

the Christmas Kitten

written by
Jessica Spawn

illustrated by
Benjamin Vincent

One Christmas Eve
on a dark lonely street,
Kitten was hungry,
he had nothing to eat.

This cold winter's night,
he went for a roam.

Wishing for a family, and a place to call home.

Suddenly he saw a bird in the sky
He watched it swoop down—
how fast it could fly!

The bird thought he'd snatch
the frightened Kitten.

Instead he saw
DASHER,
PRANCER,
and BLITZEN!

The gallant reindeer
from Santa's pack
Appeared, and stood tall
behind Kitten's back.

Deciding it was not worth the fight,
The bird fluttered away into the dark night.

The reindeer gathered
  'round this lucky guy,
Asking "Why so sad?
    What is making you cry?"

Kitten confided that he was alone,
  With nowhere to go, no place to call home.

Prancer looked at the others
with a smile and a nod,
Then he gathered two sticks
and did something quite odd:

He made tiny antlers for Kitten's head.
Not a word was spoken, not a word was said.

Prancer motioned for Kitten
to jump on his back.
They soared into the night,
toward the sky so black.

In the blink of an eye,
they were with SANTA CLAUS.
He was busy packing presents
but stopped for a pause.

He bellowed,
"WELCOME, MY FURRY
FOUR-FOOTED FRIEND!"

Then returned to loading the sleigh again.

Hearing these words, Kitten started to cry.
Filled with compassion,
Santa asked him, "*WHY?*"

"Well, Santa, it's not
only me who's alone.
There are so many
kittens in need
of a home."

Santa pondered a moment,
then made a remark:
"WE SHALL FIX IT THIS CHRISTMAS.
TONIGHT WE MUST START!"

They mapped out places
    where kittens would roam,
Ones needing a family
    and home of their own.

When they finished their task,
    Santa smiled and said,
"TOMORROW THE MAGIC,
    BUT NOW TIME FOR BED."

Prancer cuddled with Kitten under his arm,
As the reindeer slept in their cozy barn.

Kitten was much too excited to fall asleep.
But he did not move, he did not make a peep.

He wished, and he willed, and he wiggled his whiskers.
Hoping that Christmas would get here much quicker.

Finally Kitten closed his sweet eyes.
In a flash, he awoke—Christmas day had arrived!

Santa summoned his reindeer to start their big day.
Ready to ride, Kitten hopped in his sleigh.

They stopped everywhere that was marked on their map,
And rescued each sweet little homeless cat.

Then all the homes in every town, land, and city,
Received a PURRfectly matched happy little kitty.

Now all the kittens would indeed have a home.
A place to be loved, a place they could roam.

A family to snuggle
       and kiss them goodnight,
Free to romp and to pounce,
       to purr and play-fight.

Kitten realized that the world was at peace.
Then he kissed every reindeer
from the first to the least.

He went to thank Santa,
who was eating some cookies.
Santa winked and shared milk
while no one was looking.

Kitten snuggled down deep
in the lap of Mrs. Claus,
And made happy kitty feet
with his happy kitty paws.

MEEEOOOOW

PURR

Purring and twitching
 is how this story ends,
For cat-loving homes
 all across the lands.

MEEOOW

This is the story
        of that magical night,
When Kitten's wish
        changed everyone's life.

THE END

About the PAWthor

Jessica Spawn is a "cat mom" of three fur babies and loves all things cats! She is a filmmaker and entrepreneur who is passionate about sharing PURRpose with others and helping create a "culture of kindness." She is a lifelong storyteller and enjoys engaging with people on various mediums and platforms as she constantly looks for ways to make people laugh!

Jessica founded Hungry Cat Media, LLC—a company that focuses on creating content that is congruent with her life themes of "Heart, Humor, and Hope." Hungry Cat Media handles content creation, social media strategies, and brand management for clients ranging from influencers to corporations.

As a filmmaker, her short film *Instagram Cat Mom* gained traction as it takes a peek into the life of the ultimate "PAWparazzi," delivering smiles as well as encouraging a love for kitties! Taking on this PURRsona of "Instagram Cat Mom" allows her to run around being ridiculously aMEOWzing and have a blast encouraging others to love their cats and just enjoy the journey of life.

For more cat-themed fun, and to join Jessica's MEWsletter, visit **HungryCatMedia.com** or **InstagramCatMom.com**. FURR the cutest pics and adventures of her kitty clan and her fellow celebriCATS, PURRlease follow Jessica on Instagram (**@instacatmom**) or connect on Facebook (**@instagramcatmom**). P.S. She LOVES to receive cat photos and videos from FURRiends!

The Story Behind The Story

The Christmas Kitten was a passion project for me that came to life after the loss of a marriage along with a (co-founded) company. As a creative, it was gut wrenching for me to lay down a vision for a brand that I created and to navigate the loss of a grand idea. I was praying about it and telling God how sad this made me, and how I didn't want to feel this way about my favorite holiday. The next day I woke up and had the idea for this book. I think in the end, as I read over the story, I realized I am a bit of that little scared lonely kitten. I'm very blessed with the community who surrounded me as I walked out this season of the unknown and I want to help the next generation learn to love and share and lift each other up. I want them to know that anything is PAWsible, and I want them to grow up knowing that truly, one idea can change everyone's life.

About the Illustrator

Benjamin Vincent is a freelance illustrator based in Dallas. He began his career as a caricature artist at the age of 17 when he worked at Six Flags Over Texas one summer. Later, he traveled and studied in Europe and then attended Art Center College of Pasadena, California.

Benjamin is a story-teller at heart and was drawn to illustration as a way of telling stories through a visual medium. It's all about the story, the images take your imagination to the next level. When he's not playing with cats or running around with his pup, he illustrates for magazines and advertising agencies, is a well-known caricature artist, and enjoys illustrating children's books.

He's drawn to the challenge of telling the client's story in his work as a commercial illustrator. In the Christmas Kitty, Benjamin was touched by the story and the passion of the storyteller to tell her story.

To contact Ben for a project, visit **benvincent.com**.

A favorite PAWliday tradition is baking and decorating suPURR fun Cat-shaped cookies.

Making cookies is such a fun (and sometimes messy!) way to spend time together as a family. Everyone can get as creative as they like, the only RULE is to have FUN!

The finished masterpieces make great gifts for teachers and neighbors, or start a family tradition of delivering cookies to your local homeless shelter or to anyone who needs a little extra love at the holidays.

Happy Baking and Merry CATmas!
~*Jessica*

Visit **InstagramCatMom.com** for recipe and tips.

Thank MEW to a magical team,
who came together to help accomplish my Dream!

My Dear Daddy God—You took this scared little kitten and loved me back to life. You redeemed my losses, including the reindeer.

My Parents—You supported my dreams and championed me to the finish line for this book.

My Sister—I love our silly times and our "Christmas faces."

My Auntie Tish—My lifelong cheerleader. You are the reason I am a writer!

My Friends and Family—You believed in me and lent me your faith. You texted me, called me, and cheered me on. You became the momentum I needed to actually DO my DREAM!

My 3 kitty loves: Gracie, Bordeaux, and Bungie—You are my daily insPURRation for this grand adventure called life!

Benjamin Vincent—My masterful illustrator, you read my words, and SAW my vision. This book would not be the same without you. You said yes to this "hungry cat" and made it PAWsible! benvincent.com

Andra Dunn—You #girlboss I adore you! You rock web design and social media! Thanks for all you do and I look forward to many projects ahead! convertible-communications.com

David Pollock—Thank you for being my cinematographer and editing the footage I used in the marketing of this book! Looking forward to a film project soon!

Brooke Sailer—You shared your experience on how you self published. You sat with me over coffee and helped me brainstorm. You opened your heart and shared your time! Thank MEW. brookesailer.com

Amy Betz—You helped me where I needed it most... details! For all the punctuation, and the re-editing you helped me with when I kept changing my mind on the story. tinytalesediting.com

Paul and Katrina Sirmon—Y'all GET meow! You saw the vision when I cast it and you made this story come alive! You took a complete amateur and made me an author. Kat, thank MEW especially for you're extra special feedback and for the FURRst lines of the book :) Ya'll are PAWsome! buzzbombcreative.com

Melissa Lapierre—Thank you for your blog interMEW and your constant encouragement online! mochasmysteriesmeows.com

Cindy at The Casual Cat Cafe—I love teaming up to make DFW the hot spot for cat lovers! thecasualcatcafe.com

All my "Instagram Cat Mom" fans and friends—Thanks for doing this crazy cat lady life with meow!

Stella—My "bestie." Thank you for helping me through the hardest season of my life.

All my CAT-sistants—You worked FURR nothing other than to support my PAWparazzi vision. I love you. I'm deeply and eternally grateful.

Made in the USA
Monee, IL
04 April 2021